Walt Disney's
The Ugly Duckling

Story adapted by **Monique Peterson**
Pictures by **The Walt Disney Studios**
Adapted by **Don MacLaughlin**

A WELCOME BOOK

EDITIONS

New York

IN THE HEART OF THE BEAUTIFUL COUNTRYSIDE lived a mother duck. Her nest was in the loveliest spot under a big, shady tree. She longed to stretch her legs and go for a swim in the warm summer sun. But instead she sat patiently, waiting for her five eggs to hatch.

After many long and quiet days, Mother Duck
heard a pecking sound. Could it be time?

"Quack! Quack!" she cried and hopped off
her nest to peek at the eggs. One wiggled.
Another wobbled. The pecking sounds got
louder and louder. *Crack-crack-crack-crack!* Out
popped one...two...three...*four* fuzzy ducklings!

The downy youngsters scrambled out of their
shells as quickly as their webbed feet could waddle.
"Look how big and bright the world is!" they
peeped as they explored all around their nest.

"The world is far bigger than this, my children."
Mother Duck smiled. "Follow me and we'll go for
a refreshing swim in the lake."

Before she could lead her ducklings to the
water, Mother Duck remembered the fifth egg.
"Oh, dear!" she cried. "The biggest egg of all
still hasn't hatched. Hmph!" she snorted grumpily.

"It's probably a turkey egg," she muttered. "Oh, well. I sat this long, I might as well sit a bit longer." And so, Mother Duck settled back down on the biggest egg.

Finally, after a very long time, the big egg
began to wiggle and wobble. Mother Duck and
her precious ducklings gathered around the nest
to watch. At last, *crrrrack!* The new hatchling
broke out of his shell!

What a sight he was! He looked nothing like his
brothers and sisters. Instead of sunshiny yellow,
he was a dull gray. And he was awfully big.

"Honk! Honk!" he greeted his new family.

But his brothers and sisters weren't so friendly.

"You're *ugly*!" quacked the ducklings.

"Yes," agreed Mother Duck. "You must be a turkey after all. All my other children are the spitting image of their father." Then Mother Duck turned her back on the big hatchling and quacked to the others. "Come along children, we've waited long enough to go for a swim."

"Quack! Quack! Quack!" piped the youngsters. "We don't want to swim with such an ugly duckling!"

The Ugly Duckling wanted to swim, too. He followed the others to the lake and floated easily on the surface. The cool water felt so refreshing on his big floppy feet!

"Look, Mom! I can swim, too!" he called. But Mother
Duck and the ducklings swam away and pretended
not to notice him.

So the Ugly Duckling found himself all alone on the big lake. Heartbroken, he swam to a quiet spot among the marshy reeds. There, hidden from the rest of the world, the poor duckling drooped his head and cried and cried and cried. Big, sad tears splashed into the lake.

As the Ugly Duckling looked at the ripples each teardrop made in the water, he saw a horrible sight—a terrible, twisted face looking right back at him. It was his own reflection.

"I *am* ugly!" he cried. "No wonder no one wants to be near me!" And he covered his eyes from his image and felt more alone than before.

The Ugly Duckling decided to run far, far away where no one would be bothered by his ugliness. He waddled through fields and glens deep into the forest.

Finally, he came upon a clearing where he
saw a nest of young birds chirping happily away.
Maybe they'll be my friends, he thought. And
for the first time, he felt hopeful.

The Ugly Duckling climbed into the tree. "Cheep, cheep, cheep, cheep!" the baby birds greeted him. "Come play with us. Mother is returning soon with food. She'll be happy to have you in our nest."

"Thank you!" honked the Ugly Duckling. How wonderful it would be to have a mother who would welcome him! He played with his new brothers and sisters and waited patiently for Mother Bird.

Soon, Mother Bird came home with a fat, juicy worm in her mouth. The Ugly Duckling had forgotten how hungry he was and snapped the worm right out of Mother Bird's beak and swallowed it whole.

"Squawk, squawk, squawk!" scolded Mother Bird. "Shame on you, you big ugly thing! How dare you take food from my babies!" And she shooed him out of her nest and far away from her children.

The Ugly Duckling had to keep running so he wouldn't get snapped in the tail by the angry mother bird.

The Ugly Duckling wandered for many lonely hours until he came to a large pond.

There, floating among the reeds, he saw the biggest, friendliest-looking duck he'd ever seen. "Perhaps he won't mind that I'm so ugly," he said hopefully. So he swam timidly toward the colorful mallard.

The big duck didn't swim away or call him names! He simply smiled warmly.

The Ugly Duckling snuggled close to his newfound friend. He was so overcome with happiness, he didn't even notice that the mallard wasn't a duck at all. He was nothing more than painted wood.

The Ugly Duckling nudged the smiling decoy. "Let's play!" he honked.

The wooden duck bobbed his head up and down and up and down.

"At last! Someone wants to play with me!" Excited, the duckling climbed onto the big duck's back and jumped into the water. *Splash!* What fun!

And he continued to splash and play, filling
the pond with waves. The decoy bobbed back
and forth more and more until . . . *BONK!* Its big,
wooden bill hit the Ugly Duckling smack-dab in
the middle of his forehead!

The Ugly Duckling paddled to safety as quickly as he could. "He must have attacked me because I'm so ugly," he wailed.

Then the sad little duckling suddenly realized he would have to spend the rest of his life all alone. The thought hurt him more than a bump on his head ever could. And he flopped on the log and cried his little heart out.

Out of the blue, he heard a *honk-honk-honk*ing
all around him. He looked up and saw the most
wonderful sight of all! A flock of magnificent
young birds gathered around him.

He thought they were the loveliest creatures
he'd ever seen. If only he could be half as lovely!

He was so elated to have company that he dove all the way to the bottom of the pond. But when he popped up at the surface, he found himself alone once again.

The other birds were paddling away, *honk-honk-honk*ing in the distance.

Why should I think that they would want to play with me? he thought gloomily.

Just when he thought he would be alone and miserable forever, something amazing happened! The beautiful birds returned. And with them swam the most glorious bird in the world.

"Look, Mother!" honked the happy cygnets. "We've found a new brother!"

The Ugly Duckling couldn't believe his eyes or his ears.

"You're home, now, little one," said the mother swan as she cradled the Ugly Duckling under her snowy white wing. "You are a fine young swan."

From the shore, Mother Duck and her ducklings watched the graceful swan welcome the Ugly Duckling into her family.

As he swam away with his new family, he ruffled his feathers and held his head up high. Never before had the Ugly Duckling felt so much love in his heart.